STAR WARS

ADVENTURES IN
HYPERSPACE

DOWN

m
rary District
O

C.

Auckland
Sydney   Mexico City   New Delhi   Hong Kong

DISCARD

BY

BERTHOUD COMMUNITY
LIBRARY DISTRICT

ISBN 978-0-545-21359-2

12 11 10 9 8 7 6 5 4 3 2 1   10 11 12 13 14 15/0

Cover and interior illustrations by Robert Rath
Printed in the U.S.A.   40
First printing, June 2010

A hushed silence fell over the spectators as the two monsters entered the arena. One was a native of the planet Tatooine. The other wasn't. Both were immense beasts with sharp claws and powerful jaws. And both were very hungry.

Jabba the Hutt, watching from his private box, laughed as he tossed out a raw bantha leg. It was a good throw. The meat landed in the center of the arena floor, between the two monsters.

The monsters eyed each other and snarled. The native squill was a deadly carnivore with a green leathery hide. Jabba's swoop gang had captured the squill after it made the mistake of straying from its desert cave.

The squill's opponent was a red-skinned gundark. Bringing the gundark to Tatooine had not

been easy, but as Jabba surveyed the excited crowd, he was glad he had made the effort.

The monsters lunged at each other. Most of the spectators shouted enthusiastically. Others cringed, fearing they were about to lose their money. Jabba laughed heartily because he knew he could only win. After all, he owned the arena.

Jabba's arena was located in the Desilijic Complex, the Hutt's sprawling property at Mos Eisley Spaceport on Tatooine. Jabba also controlled most of the gambling in Mos Eisley, among other things.

The squill pounced and sank its teeth into one of the gundark's four arms. The gundark howled and flung the squill to the ground. The squill rolled to its feet and sprang back at the gundark.

"Haw!" Jabba cried with glee. He reached into his snack bowl, pulled out two wriggling dyadworms, and popped them into his mouth.

Jabba was not alone in his private box. Two Gamorreans, both carrying large axes, and three blaster-wielding bodyguards stood

close by. Jabba's assistant, the Twi'lek Bib Fortuna, lurked in the shadows at the back of the box.

Then Han Solo and Chewbacca the Wookiee
arrived. Jabba's bodyguards had been expecting the pair, and made no move to stop them.
Brushing past Bib Fortuna, Han said, "Having fun,
Jabba?"

"I *always* have fun, Solo," Jabba said, keeping his slit-pupil eyes on the battling monsters.

"That's great," Han replied sarcastically, raising his voice so the Hutt could hear him over the noisy crowd.

Another howl came from the arena floor. Chewbacca could not help watching the fight with some interest. He'd never seen a squill go up against a gundark. He suddenly found himself rooting for the gundark, who — like the Wookiee himself — was far from home.

2

The gundark swung its upper arms at the squill. The squill ducked and then leaped onto the gundark's back. Wrapping its arms around its opponent's neck, the squill then bit the gundark's ear.

As the spectators shouted from their seats, Han kept his eyes on Jabba. "You invited me here to talk business, remember?"

"No, Solo. I have not forgotten about our business meet —" The Hutt was interrupted by a loud *snap* from the arena floor.

"Haw-haw!" Jabba burst with laughter. "Did you see what the newcomer just did to the hometown favorite?!"

"No, but I *heard*," Han said without pleasure. "So . . . about business?"

Jabba pointed to the gundark. "*That* monster killed three of my Gamorrean guards. Fortunately, new guards and a large supply of food await pickup on Gamorr."

"Gamorr, huh?" Han glanced at Jabba's guards. "Gamorreans don't exactly encourage visitors."

"No, they do not," Jabba said. "And my contact on Gamorr does not trust strangers. For these reasons, I must insist you bring my best translator."

"A translator? Can't you just tell your contact that *you* trust me?"

The Hutt smiled. "You amuse me, Solo. The translator will meet you at your docking bay. Bib Fortuna will give you all the other details." Jabba wiggled his stubby fingers, signaling his assistant to step forward.

Bib Fortuna had been lurking at the back of Jabba's box. He moved beside Han and held out a datacard.

Han ignored Bib and the extended datacard. "Not so fast, Jabba," Han said. "How much does this job *pay*?"

Bib Fortuna did not like being ignored. Leaning close to Han, the Twi'lek bared his sharp teeth and hissed, "*I* tell you the payment! You *will* accept! No haggling!"

Han kept his eyes locked on the Hutt. "I'd better warn you, Jabba, my price goes up if Brain-tails doesn't start using mouthwash."

Embarrassed, Bib Fortuna raised a hand over his mouth and tried to smell his own breath. Jabba chuckled and said, "Five thousand credits."

Han shook his head. "Eight thousand."

Just then, another bone-crunching sound was followed by a monster's yowl from the arena floor. The spectators went wild, and Jabba's watchful, bulbous eyes grew wide with delight. "That *had* to hurt," he said. "Six thousand credits."

"I *might* agree to seven thousand," Han said, "if I knew there was a higher-paying job waiting for me when I got back."

Looking away from the carnage on the arena floor, Jabba smiled at Han. "Six thousand, five hundred. And after you return from Gamorr, I *might* hire you for a long-haul . . . perhaps to Wild Space."

"Wild Space, huh?" Han glanced at Chewbacca. The Wookiee nodded. "All right, Jabba. It's a deal." Han plucked the datacard from Bib Fortuna's hand and tucked it into his vest pocket. "I'll need three thousand in advance for expenses."

Bib looked at his boss. The Hutt nodded. Bib reached into a belt pouch and removed three silver-plated credit chips. Handing the chips to Han, Bib sneered and said, "I did not know riffraff had expenses!"

"And I had no idea you could count to three, Brain-tails," Han said with a grin. "C'mon, Chewie."

Chewbacca looked at Han and answered with a bark.

Han replied, "No, we *can't* stay and watch the fight. We have to prep the *Falcon!*"

Before Chewbacca could protest, a sickening

thud came from below. The Wookiee returned his gaze to the arena floor, and saw the gundark had flattened the squill. Chewbacca tilted his head back and roared.

Han said, "Happy now?"

Chewbacca nodded. Then he snarled at Bib Fortuna, just to make the Twi'lek jump, before he followed Han out of Jabba's box.

Han and Chewbacca made their way to the
arena's exit. As they stepped out into the baking
heat, the Wookiee grunted bitterly.

"I don't want Gamorreans on the *Falcon*, either,
pal," Han answered. "They smell worse than Bib
Fortuna's breath. I'm also not thrilled about Jabba
insisting that we take a translator."

Chewbacca shrugged, then let out a whimper.

"You're *always* hungry!" Han replied. "If we're
lucky, maybe the translator knows how to cook."

Chewbacca responded with a hopeful growl.

Docking Bay 94 was just a short walk from Jabba's arena at Mos Eisley Spaceport. Han Solo's ship, the *Millennium Falcon*, was inside the open-roofed docking bay. Han was in the *Falcon*, making an adjustment to the hyperdrive's horizontal booster.

Chewbacca barked loudly from outside the ship. Han yelled back, "Tell the translator I'll be right out!"

Han set aside his tools and stepped down the *Falcon*'s landing ramp. When he saw Jabba's translator, he said, "Oh, you've got to be kidding me."

The translator was a droid, an old Cybot Galactica protocol unit with a faded green head and body. Chewbacca noticed Han's surprised expression and let out a braying laugh.

"Hello, Captain Solo," the droid said in a female voice. "My name is TC-72. Master Jabba has instructed me to travel with you to Gamorr."

Han scowled. "I don't care what your instructions are," he said. "Jabba should have known better than to send a droid."

Confused, TC-72 said, "May I ask why, sir?"

"Because I don't like machines that talk back!"

"Oh," said TC-72 sadly. "I'm very sorry that you feel that way, Captain."

"Listen, droid. Go back to Jabba, and tell him to send a *breathing* translator."

"I'm sorry, sir," TC-72 said, "but I'm afraid I can't do that."

Losing his patience, Han said, "Do you understand the word 'scram'?"

"Yes, sir," TC-72 said. "I meant to say I *can* go back to Jabba, but I can't tell him to send another translator. Master Jabba told me that if

you refused to take me to Gamorr, he would hire BoShek instead."

"BoShek?" Han said with surprise. "But I —"

TC-72 interrupted, "Master Jabba also instructed me to collect your advance of three thousand credits, plus fifty percent interest, as stipulated in the datacard you received from Bib Fortuna."

Han gasped. "Fifty percent?!"

TC-72 nodded. "Do you wish to pay Jabba personally?"

"I don't prefer to pay Jabba *ever!*" Han fumed. "Just . . . get on board!"

"Yes, sir," TC-72 said as she walked toward the *Falcon*'s landing ramp. "Goodness, I've never traveled on such an old ship. Are you certain it will reach Gamorr?"

Han shook his head and muttered, "Why me?"

Chewbacca chuckled.

While Chewbacca went to the *Falcon*'s cockpit to prepare for liftoff, Han led TC-72 to the main hold. Han said, "Sit there, and buckle up." He gestured to the seat that curved around the built-in hologame table.

TC-72 looked at the seat. "I might be of more use to you in the cockpit, sir. I could tell you about Gamorrean history and culture, so when we arrive on Gamorr, you'll be fully informed about —"

"I said," Han interrupted, "*sit there!*"

TC-72 lowered herself onto the seat beside the hologame table while Han stepped over to the engineering station. Reaching for a safety belt, TC-72 found the metal buckle was slightly cracked. Then she noticed some wires and cables dangling out of the ceiling's maintenance hatch.

"Dear me," TC-72 said. "Do you realize that this vessel is in violation of numerous safety codes?

You really should have an inspector conduct a thorough —"

"That does it." Han turned from the engineering station and moved toward the seated droid. TC-72 saw he was carrying a small toolbox.

Three minutes later, Han joined Chewbacca in the cockpit. Chewbacca had already started the *Falcon*'s engines. Han said, "All set?"

Chewbacca nodded. The *Falcon*'s thrusters fired, and then the ship began rising out of the docking bay. As they traveled up and away from Mos Eisley, the Wookiee barked a question.

Han replied, "How would I know if the droid can play hologames?! But if you ask her between here and Gamorr, don't expect an answer!"

Now there's something you don't see everyday, Chewie," Han Solo said. "Mushrooms taking an afternoon stroll!"

Chewbacca answered with a chuckling hoot as the dome-capped fungi moved across the ground.

"Now that you mention it, pal," Han replied, "I don't believe I've ever seen it at *any* time of day."

Han and Chewbacca were so amused that they almost forgot about the four hulking Gamorreans who had led them to the mushrooms. Growing impatient, one Gamorrean — a farmer — snorted rudely.

Han and Chewbacca had not had any difficulty traveling through hyperspace to the planet Gamorr. Using the datacard that Bib Fortuna had given him, Han had easily located the mushroom farm at the edge of a large forest. They had landed the *Millennium Falcon* in a clearing beside the farm.

Jabba's contact turned out to be the farmer, who wore a ragged leather tunic. The three other Gamorreans were the new guards that Jabba had hired. Although the Gamorreans had been expect-

ing Han and Chewbacca, they did nothing to make the travelers feel welcome. The farmer snorted again, this time more loudly.

Chewbacca ignored the farmer and continued to watch the mushrooms. Han turned to face the farmer. "I don't suppose you speak Basic?"

The farmer spat, launching a stream of yellowish fluid that came dangerously close to the toe of Han's left boot.

"I'll take that as a 'No'."

Han turned to Chewbacca. "I'd hoped we could avoid using the droid that Jabba insisted we bring here. But it looks like we've got no choice." He reached to his belt, removed a droid caller, and activated the device. A moment later, TC-72 came trotting down the *Millennium Falcon*'s landing ramp. Han waved and said, "Over here, motormouth!"

Seeing Han, TC-72 gave a muffled reply, then began walking toward the group.

The Gamorreans' beady eyes blinked at the sight of the approaching droid. When TC-72 came to a stop in front of Han, the Gamorreans saw why the droid's voice had sounded muffled. A thin, rectangular magnetic plate had been secured over the droid's mouth.

Facing the droid, Han said, "Now, I'm pretty sure you *finally* understand what I told you earlier? About how I don't like machines that talk too much?"

TC-72 nodded.

"Good," Han said. "Then we'll get along fine." He reached up and peeled off the magnetic plate from the droid's face.

TC-72 tilted her head slightly and made a rasp-
ing sound to test her audio output. Han thought
TC-72 was about to say something, so he held up
the magnetic plate and dangled it in front of the
droid's face. Han said, "Don't even think of thank-
ing me for letting you speak again!"

TC-72's head jerked back slightly, but she remained silent.

Han gestured to the mushroom farmer. "Ask this guy if the food shipment that Jabba ordered is ready for pickup."

TC-72 turned to face the Gamorrean clad in ragged leathers. "Oh," said TC-72. Then she turned back to face Han and said, "Sir, I believe there's something I should first tell you about —"

"No," Han interrupted. "Chewie and I heard *enough* of your comments and observations before we even left Tatooine! Right, Chewie?"

Chewbacca kept his eyes on the snoruuks, but responded with a low growl.

"Oh, my," TC-72 said nervously. "However, I really do believe you should be aware that —"

"Ask him about the mushrooms!" Han snapped.

Returning her attention to the Gamorrean, TC-72 made a series of grunting noises. The Gamorrean grunted in response, and then pointed to a nearby stone building with a wide door.

TC-72 turned to Han and translated, "The shipment of mushrooms — they're called *snoruuks* — is on a sledge in that shed. Would you like the three guards to haul them to your ship?"

"Naw, Chewie can handle it," Han said. "Right, Chewie?" But when he looked at his friend, he found the Wookiee had scooped up a snoruuk. Chewbacca chortled as the fungus moved across the palm of his furry hand.

"Stop playing with the merchandise," Han said. "It's not professional!"

Chewbacca whimpered as he put down the snoruuk. Then he rose and walked over to the stone building. He pushed the door open to reveal a sledge that carried several cargo containers. Each container was filled with snoruuks.

Chewbacca gripped the sledge's handles and began hauling it toward the *Falcon*'s landing ramp. As he walked past Han, he barked a question.

"No, you *can't* keep a snoruuk," Han said, rolling his eyes.

Chewbacca whimpered again.

Han, TC-72, and the Gamorreans followed Chewbacca over to the *Falcon*. While Chewbacca transferred the cargo into the ship, Han called out to TC-72. "Hey, droid. Tell the farmer that I'm happy to bring these mushrooms to Tatooine. Tell him it *pleases* me that Jabba's guards will be eating well, and that I've enjoyed doing business with him."

TC-72 hesitated for a moment, but then she made more guttural noises at the farmer. The Gamorrean responded with a snort and several grunts. Looking at Han, TC-72 said, "The farmer wonders if you have anything to trade."

Han beamed. "That's what I was hoping he'd say. Tell him I have two bolts of Trevella cloth and a bantha hide. Find out how much he's interested, and also what he's got for trade."

TC-72 grunted at the farmer. The Gamorrean answered with an angry snort, and then spat at the ground again. TC-72 looked at Han. "I believe that means 'Not interested'."

Baffled, Han said, "But the stuff's good! Ask him . . . no, *tell* him the cloth would be a great gift . . . maybe for his wife or mother?"

TC-72 glanced at the Gamorrean farmer, but then shook her head. "The farmer made it quite clear that —"

"I'm not asking for your opinion," Han said. "Ask him if he knows any female Gamorreans who need some fabric."

"But, sir, I'm afraid that would —"

"Ask him!"

TC-72 made a sound that resembled a sad sigh. Then she faced the Gamorrean and translated Han's question. To Han's surprise, all four Gamorreans responded with angry sputters. Then the farmer squealed and threw a hard, backhanded slap at TC-72's head.

The droid's head snapped free from her neck and fell away from her body, which remained standing. Han watched TC-72's head bounce before it rolled to a stop beside one leg of the *Falcon*'s landing gear.

Han stared at TC-72's head, which was facing the sky. Han asked, "Why'd he hit you?"

TC-72's head replied, "Because, sir . . . as I was trying to tell you . . . the farmer is a *female*."

The Gamorreans stomped their feet. The farmer shook a massive fist at Han. Han said, "Oh. Can you tell her that you, uh, translated my words wrong?"

"Only if you promise not to leave me here . . . *sir*."

Han picked up TC-72's head. As the droid began apologizing to the farmer, Chewbacca stepped down from the *Falcon*'s landing ramp. The Wookiee saw the decapitated droid, and then noticed how all four Gamorreans were glaring at Han. Chewbacca barked a question.

"No, Chewie. Everything's under control. But if you're done loading the cargo, give me a hand with the droid. I hate to admit it, but she just saved my neck."

As the *Millennium Falcon* rose away from the planet Gamorr, Chewbacca threw back his head and let out a braying laugh.

Seated in the cockpit beside Chewbacca, Han shook his head with disbelief. "You knew the farmer was a female? And you didn't *tell* me?"

Chewbacca's laugh became a honking bark.

"Yeah, really funny," Han muttered as he adjusted the flight controls. "If the farmer had taken my head off instead of the droid's, that would have been a riot."

The *Falcon* left Gamorr's atmosphere and entered space. A few minutes later, Chewbacca angled the ship toward the nearest hyperspace portal. Han said, "Coordinates are set for the jump to Tatooine?"

Chewbacca nodded. Han pressed a switch to activate the *Falcon*'s hyperdrive. Outside the cockpit, the surrounding stars appeared to suddenly elongate and extend past the ship. But just as the *Falcon* leaped into hyperspace, a loud crash of metal echoed from the main hold.

Han said, "Didn't you tell me the passengers were belted in?"

Chewbacca answered with a moaning bark.

"Well, putting the Gamorreans in the main hold wasn't my idea," Han said as he scrambled out of his seat. "The droid said she'd make sure they behaved themselves."

Chewbacca followed Han out of the cockpit, leaving the computer systems in control of the *Falcon*'s journey. As they ran through the passage tube that led to the main hold, they heard another crash from ahead. Although they had dealt with many problems on their ship before, neither was prepared for the sight that waited for them.

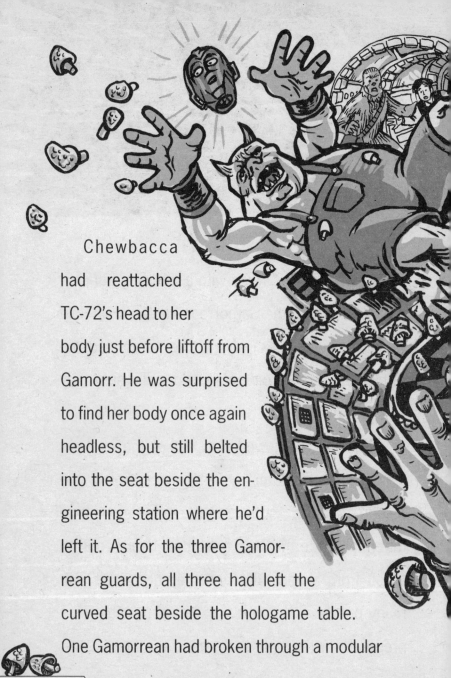

Chewbacca had reattached TC-72's head to her body just before liftoff from Gamorr. He was surprised to find her body once again headless, but still belted into the seat beside the engineering station where he'd left it. As for the three Gamorrean guards, all three had left the curved seat beside the hologame table. One Gamorrean had broken through a modular wall panel to get to the shipment of snoruuks in the freight-loading room, and let loose a few hundred snoruuks. The other two Gamorreans were playing catch with TC-72's head.

Han gasped. "My ship!"

And then Chewbacca noticed the hologame table's surface was cracked.

The outraged Wookiee roared.

Chewbacca's roar startled the Gamorreans. TC-72's head fell past one Gamorrean's outstretched hands and landed upon a cluster of moving mushrooms. Han stepped past the snoruuks and grabbed TC-72's head. "You said the guards would behave!"

"It appears I was mistaken," TC-72 replied. "But I don't believe they meant any harm. They're relatively young Gamorreans, and still very playful."

"Playful? Have you looked at yourself lately?" Han held TC-72's head so her photoreceptors could view the wires sticking out of the neck of her seated body.

"Oh, my," TC-72 said. "I believe my logic circuits have been damaged."

"Some help *you* are. How about your translator functions? Are they still working?"

"Yes, sir."

"Tell the guards to clean up this mess," Han said, "and if they don't do a good job, Chewbacca will be eating roasted Gamorreans for dinner."

TC-72's head translated Han's words to the guards. The Gamorreans looked nervously at the Wookiee, then bent down and began scooping up the snoruuks as fast as they could.

After all the snoruuks were returned to the cargo containers, Chewbacca locked the Gamorreans up in one of the Falcon's smaller holds. He rejoined Han in the main hold. Han handed TC-72's head to Chewbacca and said, "See if you can fix her again, so she's in one piece when we meet Jabba."

Chewbacca glanced at the cracked hologame table and whimpered.

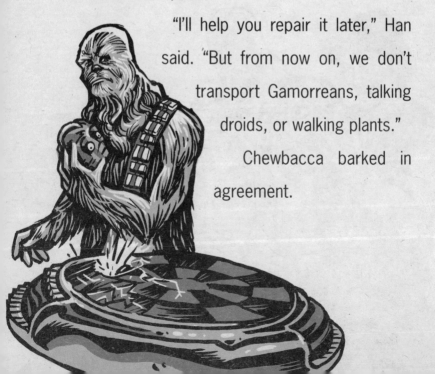

"I'll help you repair it later," Han said. "But from now on, we don't transport Gamorreans, talking droids, or walking plants."

Chewbacca barked in agreement.

Jabba the Hutt was sitting in his private box at his arena on Tatooine, watching his prized gundark fight off a group of unusually large womp rats, when Han Solo and Chewbacca arrived. It was the day after the *Millennium Falcon* had returned from Gamorr with Jabba's new guards and the snoruuk shipment. As Han and Chewbacca approached Jabba, they noticed TC-72 standing beside Bib Fortuna at the back of the box.

"All right, Jabba," Han said. "You mentioned a Wild Space job?"

Jabba plucked a three-eyed gorg from a jar. He tossed the gorg into his mouth and swallowed it whole. Then he looked at Han and said, "As I recall, I told you I *might* hire you for a long-haul to Wild Space. But first, we have to settle a small matter of what you owe me for your trip to Gamorr."

"Excuse me? Did you just say *I* owe *you*?"

"You heard me, Solo," Jabba said. "You went to Gamorr because you were working for me. However, while on Gamorr, you attempted to conduct your own trade with the snoruuk farmer, who was my contact. It is my understanding that you offered her two bolts of Trevella cloth and a bantha hide."

"How'd you hear about —" Before Han finished his question, he suddenly knew the answer. He looked at TC-72. The droid gazed back at him and shrugged. Han sneered and said, "Well, aren't *you* the chatty one?"

Returning his attention to Jabba, Han said, "Did your droid happen to mention that your lovely Gamorrean contact had no interest in any of the stuff I was offering?"

Jabba made a clucking sound at the back of his throat. "Han, my boy, did you *read* the data-card that Bib Fortuna gave to you before you left for Gamorr?"

"Sure," Han said. "I mean, I read *most* of it."

Jabba smiled. "Then you *know* I require a small fee from anyone — even friends like you — who wants permission to conduct business with my contacts."

"Friends, huh?" Han said. "I'm so glad we're not enemies. So, how much is this fee of yours?"

"Ten thousand credits," Jabba said.

Han and Chewbacca were stunned. Chewbacca gasped. Han said, "Ten?"

"What can I say?" Jabba said. "I am a generous fellow! And because we are friends, I will simply deduct this sum from your next job."

"You're too kind," Han said through clenched teeth.

Just then, a terrible screech came from the arena floor. Chewbacca's eyes flicked to the fight below. He was glad to see the gundark now had only one opponent.

"So tell us, Jabba," Han continued. "What's the Wild Space job, and how much will you pay *after* the deduction?"

Jabba gestured to Bib Fortuna, who stepped forward and handed a new datacard to Han. "Deliver seeds and soil to Shinbone, and bring back some gems for me. You'll receive five thousand credits. No haggling."

Han frowned at the offer. "The seeds don't *walk*, do they?"

"No," Jabba chuckled. "No snoruuks this time. And you won't need a translator either."

"Fine," Han said as he pocketed the datacard. "Let's go, Chewie."

As the *Millennium Falcon* traveled through hyperspace, Chewbacca grumbled.

"I'm not happy about this job either, pal," Han replied as he readied the ship's controls for the hyperspace exit. "Flying for Jabba is becoming a real pain. Our ship smells like a greenhouse."

The smell came from the *Falcon*'s cargo, which included ten metric tons of soil and seeds. Chewbacca grunted, then barked a question.

Han replied, "No, I don't know what kind of seeds we're delivering. I never asked."

The *Falcon* dropped out of hyperspace. The ship had arrived in orbit over the planet Shinbone. Shinbone was a mining colony world in the Instrop sector, part of the vast region known as Wild Space, which was mostly unexplored. Because Shinbone was far from any major hyperspace route, the journey from Tatooine had required several stops and detours.

Han placed a datacard — the one Bib Fortuna had given him — into a slot on the navigational console, and a readout appeared on the console's datascreen. Han said, "The shipment goes to a guy named Torkil Mux.

Jabba is funding Mux's mining operation. Mux should have fifty kilograms of gems for us to bring back to Jabba. There's our destination."

Chewbacca looked at the coordinates on the datascreen, and then they began their descent.

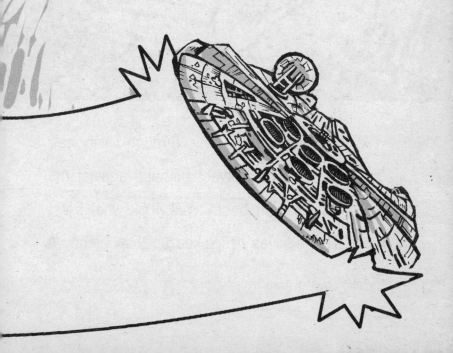

As the *Falcon* angled down through Shinbone's atmosphere, a small object bumped against the back of Han's right boot. "Well, look what I just found," Han said as he picked up the object. "A stowaway!"

Chewbacca turned his head to see Han holding a small, wiggling snoruuk.

"I wonder what it tastes like," Han said. He raised the snoruuk to his mouth, and was about to bite into it when Chewbacca roared angrily, startling Han.

"Sorry, pal. Did you want the first bite?"

The Wookiee roared again, then barked at his friend. Han replied, "You're being ridiculous, Chewie! Snoruuks may move around, but they're food. It's not an intelligent creature! It's just a wiggly mushroom."

Chewbacca growled and released the flight controls as he snatched the snoruuk from Han's hand. The snoruuk had stopped moving. The Wookiee tilted his head back and let out a mournful groan.

"Chewie, stop behaving like a — " Han gasped. "Oh, no! Look out!"

The *Falcon* was diving straight toward a rocky mountaintop. Chewbacca dropped the snoruuk as Han seized the flight controls. A moment later, there was an awful cracking sound as the *Falcon*'s energy shields struck a stone pinnacle. The engines whined as the ship veered away from the mountain.

Emergency lights flashed in the cockpit. "Aft port landing gear is damaged," Han shouted as he struggled to regain control of the *Falcon*. "Hold tight, this is gonna be bumpy!"

As Shinbone's surface appeared to race up at the *Falcon*, Chewbacca checked a datascreen and barked at Han.

Han looked offended. "I *am* heading for Torkil Mux's mine!"

Chewbacca activated the
Falcon's landing jets. Only five of
the ship's seven landing legs extended.
Han said, "We'll land on a slope to help bal-
ance things out." He jockeyed the controls,
guiding the ship to a touchdown on a rocky hill.

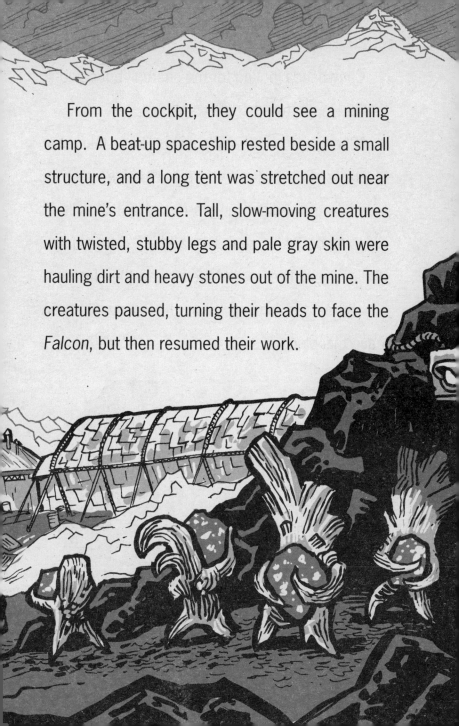

From the cockpit, they could see a mining camp. A beat-up spaceship rested beside a small structure, and a long tent was stretched out near the mine's entrance. Tall, slow-moving creatures with twisted, stubby legs and pale gray skin were hauling dirt and heavy stones out of the mine. The creatures paused, turning their heads to face the *Falcon*, but then resumed their work.

Chewbacca looked for the snoruuk but couldn't find it. He muttered sadly.

"Chewie, I know that Wookiees like to take care of plants. But in case you didn't notice, your interest in that edible fungus nearly got us killed!" Climbing out of his seat, Han added, "Come on, ya big lummox. The sooner we unload the shipment and repair the landing gear, the sooner we can leave this place."

Han stepped down the *Falcon's* landing ramp, then moved under the elevated ship to inspect the damaged landing gear. "Aw, bantha fodder! The freight elevator hatch got hammered, too. It'll take hours to fix!"

Chewie joined Han to inspect the gear. Hearing footsteps, they turned to see an Arcona and a K4 security droid approach from the structure next to the beat-up spaceship. "The Arcona must be Torkil Mux," Han said. "Stay here, Chewie, and watch my back while I talk with him."

While Chewbacca remained under the *Falcon* and kept his eyes on the security droid, Han walked up to the Arcona. "Jabba sent us for a delivery and pickup. Are you Torkil Mux?"

"I am," the Arcona replied with a slight bow. "You got here fast. I wasn't expecting you until to-morrow."

"We took some shortcuts," Han said with a shrug.

Looking at the *Falcon*, Torkil Mux asked, "Why did you land on this hill, and not closer to my camp?"

"We, uh, had some trouble with the landing gear," Han answered. "And we need to fix the freight elevator hatch before we can unload your soil and seeds. It'll take a while."

"Take your time," Mux said. He pointed to the long tent. "The shipment goes to the green-house."

Just then, a short gray-skinned worker began shifting away from the others. The K4 security droid noticed the creature's movement. Turning quickly, the droid raised its blaster-rifle arm and fired.

Watching from below the *Falcon*, Chewbacca saw the droid fire a stream of laserbolts into the ground in front of the short creature. The creature stopped, wobbled slightly, and then slowly shifted back toward the other workers. Chewbacca barked anxiously at Han.

Keeping his eyes on Torkil Mux, Han called back, "Nothing to worry about, Chewie. I'm fine."

Lowering his voice, Han said casually, "Quite a set-up you have here, Mux. Looks like you know how to keep your workers from stepping out of line."

"I couldn't have done it without Jabba's funding," Mux said with a smile. "Meet me in my headquarters when you're done, and I'll have Jabba's gems ready for you."

Torkil Mux and the K4 droid walked back to the structure that served as Mux's headquarters. Han moved under the *Falcon* and returned to Chewbacca's side. The Wookiee barked a question.

"I don't like the way Mux treats his workers, either, pal," Han replied. "But for all we know, those creatures could be dangerous criminals! Anyway, it's none of our business, and we don't get paid to ask questions. Let's just get the tools we'll need to fix the hatch and landing gear."

It took Han and Chewbacca almost three hours to make repairs. While they worked, Chewbacca paused occasionally to watch the slow-moving laborers. He could not help feeling sorry for them.

When the repairs were finished, Han said, "Mux should have Jabba's gems ready for us by now. You guard the ship while I go tell him we're ready to unload the cargo. Be right back."

As Han headed for Mux's headquarters, he kept his distance from the laborers. Even though he had told Chewbacca that the creatures might be dangerous, he thought, *They sure do look harmless.*

Inside Torkil Mux's headquarters, Han found the K4 droid standing beside Mux, who was seated behind a table. On the table was a small crate filled with gems of various sizes. Mux said, "Here are Jabba's gems. Have you unloaded the seeds and soil yet?"

"No, not yet." Han looked down at the gems. "According to the datacard I got from Jabba's assistant, Jabba is expecting a lot more gems than what you've got here."

Mux sighed. "These gems are all that I've found on Shinbone for the past three seasons. Please remind Jabba that mining takes time."

"Sure, I'll tell Jabba, but I doubt he'll be very happy about it. Hutts aren't known for their patience."

Mux sighed again. "When I get my new laborers, I'll double my efforts. Would you like my droid to carry the gems to your ship?"

"Thanks, but I can handle it." Stepping out of Mux's headquarters, crate in hand, Han thought, *Mux didn't seem very concerned about Jabba. But that's Mux's problem, not mine!*

Han was carrying the crate of gems to the *Falcon* when he noticed movement near the green-house. He was astonished to see Chewbacca following the short creature that the security droid had nearly shot earlier.

The creature led Chewbacca into the green-house. Han was about to call out to his friend when he heard the Wookiee howl.

Han dropped the gem-filled crate. By the time it hit the ground he'd already drawn his blaster and was sprinting toward his friend. Holding his blaster in front of him, he entered the greenhouse fast.

He found Chewbacca standing beside the short creature. Both were facing a row of long, raised planting beds. "Chewie!" Han called out. "I heard you howl!"

Chewbacca glanced at Han, and then reached out to push gently at Han's arm, silently urging him to lower his blaster.

Han reluctantly holstered his weapon. "You gave me a scare, pal. Why did you leave the *Falcon*?"

Chewbacca nodded toward the raised planting beds. Han followed his friend's gaze. Then he gasped.

Inside the planting beds, greenish-blue plants grew up from the dark soil. Except for their color, the plants looked exactly like the short creature that had led Chewbacca into the greenhouse.

Han thought of the shipment of soil and seeds that were still on the *Falcon*. He shook his head. "Mux told me he was getting new laborers," he said. "He just didn't bother to mention he was *growing* them."

ooking away from the bizarre plants, Chewbacca grunted at Han.

"I don't like the situation either, Chewie. But there's nothing we can —"

Chewbacca interrupted with a series of sharp barks.

"Forget it." Han turned and stepped out of the greenhouse. Chewbacca barked again as he followed Han out.

"No, Chewie!" Han answered sternly. "We're here on a *job*, remember? We did not come to Shinbone to . . . to . . . to rescue a bunch of *walking plants*."

Chewbacca grabbed Han by the upper arm, spun him around, and barked again.

"You think we should leave with soil and seeds, and take the plant people with us? Oh, that's just brilliant!" Gesturing to the small crate of gems that he'd left on the ground, Han continued, "It's bad enough that Jabba's gonna be angry because we won't have all the gems he's expecting, even though that isn't *my* fault. But if we don't do this job exactly like Jabba asked, imagine how much trouble we'll be in!"

While Han and Chewbacca argued, they did not notice the short creature who had followed them out of the greenhouse. When Han mentioned the gems, the creature moved toward Han and tugged at his sleeve. Han snapped, "What do *you* want?"

The creature began moving toward Torkil Mux's spaceship, pulling Han along with him. Han said, "Let go of me!"

Han heard Chewbacca snarl from behind. Still gripped by the creature, Han said, "What's that, Chewie? You think we should follow Shorty? Fine. Let's follow Shorty."

Shorty led them into Torkil Mux's ship. Inside, Han and Chewbacca were surprised to see many large crates filled with gems. Chewbacca looked at Han and growled.

"You said it! Looks like Torkil Mux was trying to take these gems for himself."

Chewbacca barked a question.

"All right," Han answered. "If you have a plan that will keep Jabba happy, I want to hear it."

Chewbacca explained his plan to Han. When Chewbacca was done, Han said, "Not bad, Chewie. Let's do it."

Han and Shorty exited Mux's spaceship. While Shorty shared the plan with the other laborers, Han returned to the *Falcon* and brought out the hoversled, a simple anti-gravity platform used for moving freight.

Han expected Torkil Mux to emerge from his headquarters any minute. When Mux stepped out with his security droid and saw Han using the hoversled to move an entire planting bed out of the greenhouse, Mux shouted, "Stop! What are you doing?!"

"Wookiees know a lot about plants," Han replied. "My partner told me that all of these plants were diseased. If I don't remove them from the greenhouse, they'll contaminate the new seeds and soil. You wouldn't want that to happen, would you?"

"No," Mux said, "Of course not. But why are you bringing the diseased plants to your ship?"

Han answered, "So I can get rid of them properly."

As Han was transferring the last plants from the greenhouse to the *Falcon*, Torkil Mux noticed that none of his laborers were in sight. Mux motioned for Han to stop, then asked, "Where are my workers?"

Han looked around. "Beats me. All I know is that they're not on my ship." As he spoke, he waved his right arm at the *Falcon*. He thought, *I hope Chewbacca's watching for my signal.*

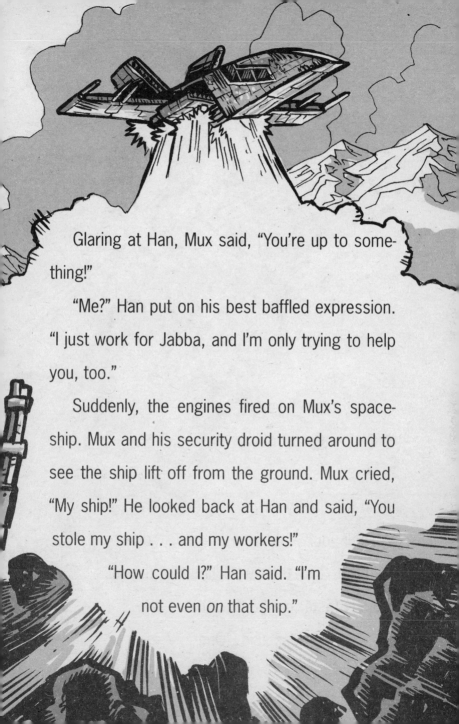

Glaring at Han, Mux said, "You're up to some-thing!"

"Me?" Han put on his best baffled expression. "I just work for Jabba, and I'm only trying to help you, too."

Suddenly, the engines fired on Mux's space-ship. Mux and his security droid turned around to see the ship lift off from the ground. Mux cried, "My ship!" He looked back at Han and said, "You stole my ship . . . and my workers!"

"How could I?" Han said. "I'm not even *on* that ship."

Mux said, "If you
don't bring my ship
back, I'll command my
droid to shoot you!"

"Tell you what," Han offered. "You count
to three, and then we'll find out if your
droid is faster on the draw than I am."

"Agreed!" Mux said. "One . . ."

Han's right hand flashed to his hip. He drew his blaster and fired at the droid. The droid's head exploded, and it collapsed to the ground.

Mux looked at his fallen droid, then said, "You cheated!"

Han shrugged. "I happen to like to shoot first," he said. "And *I'm* not the one who tried to cheat Jabba!" Han turned and walked off, taking the plants on the hoversled with him.

As soon as he was onboard the *Falcon*, Han raised the landing ramp, went to the cockpit, and started the engines. From the cockpit, he saw Torkil Mux angrily shaking a fist at him. Then the *Falcon* lifted off, and rose rapidly from Shinbone's surface.

"Chewie, do you read me?" A moment later, he heard Chewbacca's response. "Nice flying, pal," Han replied. "Prepare to dock."

Han found Mux's spaceship waiting for him in Shinbone's orbit. The two ships docked, and Chewbacca boarded the *Falcon*. Han said, "Did you and Shorty get all the plant people on board?"

Chewbacca nodded.

"Good," Han said. "Now, let's see if we can get the plant people to help us move the soil, seeds, and planting beds to the other ship, and at least

sixty kilograms of gems to the *Falcon*. Jabba's only expecting fifty kilograms of gems, so he should be more than happy."

Chewbacca barked a question.

"The rest of the gems?" Han replied. "The plant people deserve them more than we do. But where should the plant people go from here?"

Chewbacca let out a series of hoots and barks. Han answered, "Kashyyyk? You're sending the plant people to your own home planet?"

Just then, Shorty stepped up beside Chewbacca. Chewbacca growled and patted Shorty's head.

Han smiled and said, "I'm sure they'll all be very happy on Kashyyyk. Now, can we start transferring the stuff so you and I can get back to Tatooine?"

Jabba the Hutt had a private suite in his arena on Tatooine. After Han and Chewbacca delivered the gems from Shinbone, Jabba insisted that they meet with him in the suite. Jabba said, "Tell me about the mine on Shinbone."

Choosing his words carefully, Han said, "Well, after we unloaded the shipment for Torkil Mux and he gave us the gems, his droid went crazy and started shooting at everyone. Mux and his laborers fled. I shot the droid in self-defense."

Jabba's gaze traveled from Han to Chewbacca and back to Han again. Jabba said, "Mux and his laborers fled, eh? That's too bad. Those plants were unique life-forms. I just found out that the seeds that you delivered to Shinbone were the last of their kind. Very valuable."

"You mean, you knew that Mux's laborers were walking plants? That he was growing them?"

"It was Bib Fortuna's idea," Jabba said. "But if such plants run off at the first sign of trouble, what use are they to me?" Jabba reached into his snack bowl, grabbed some glowslugs, and stuffed them into his mouth. "Now," he continued, "about the gems . . ."

Han said, "What *about* the gems?"

"You brought back more than I expected, Han," Jabba said. "You could have taken some, and I might never have found out."

"Chewie and I take all sorts of risks," Han said, "but stealing from you? Give us a break, Jabba. We aren't stupid."

Jabba grinned, then bellowed, "Fortuna! Give my friend Han a credit chip so he can place a bet on the next monster fight."

Bib Fortuna handed a chip to Han. Han looked at the chip and commented, "A single credit! This must be my lucky day. Come on, Chewie. We still have to fix our hologame table."

Leaving Jabba's arena, Han and Chewie began walking back to Docking Bay 94. As they moved along the sun-baked street, Han said, "Hey, pal, I forgot to give you something." He reached into his pocket and pulled out a wriggling snoruuk.

Chewbacca cooed as he took the mushroom. Looking at Han, he barked a question.

"Of course, it's the same one you lost in the *Falcon*." Han replied. "Would I lie to *you*?"